PRINCESS
and
Minerva

by CAROLYN LANE

With illustrations by the author

SCHOLASTIC BOOK SERVICES

New York Toronto London Auckland Sydney Tokyo

In Memory of Peggy

*Books by Carolyn Lane available
through Scholastic Book Services:*

Princess
Princess and Minerva

Cover photo by Chuck Fishbein © 1981

Cover photo (top) by Creszentia Allen

ISBN 0-590-32268-0

12 11 10 9 8 7 6 5 4 3 2 1   1   2 3 4 5 6/8

Printed in the U.S.A.   01

Contents

A Moonlight Hunt   1

Danny   11

The Steel Table   18

Minerva Caged   25

Mrs. Weatherington   35

Escape   47

Minerva and the Mice   58

Home   66

A Moonlight Hunt

"She's here! She's here!" Mary Ellen's voice, shouting up over the porch railing, was shrill with excitement. "Come see, everybody! Patches is here!"

Underneath the house, in the dark corner that had been her home for as long as she could remember, Minerva blinked abruptly awake. Patches — yes! The name Mary Ellen had given her last summer, describing her spectacular, all-over calico markings. Patches. Not her real name — and not the prettiest one in the world either, come to think of it — but it didn't really matter. After the long, lonely winter it was good just to hear a human voice calling her at all.

"I can't believe it, Patches!" The round, familiar face, pressed to the trelliswork that surrounded the lower part of the house, was bright with surprise and joy. "Imagine! A

1

whole winter alone — and you're still here!"

Well, of course she was here, thought Minerva, rising and stretching. Where else would she be? This was *home*!

"Come on out now, Patches. Come on out and I'll give you some milk."

Milk!

In a flash Minerva was heading for the slatted wall, wriggling out underneath. Milk! She had nearly forgotten the taste of it — and she had nearly forgotten, too, how pleasant it was to be patted and tickled behind the ears. She didn't even mind when Mary Ellen picked her up, cuddling her, gently rocking her back and forth, carrying her up the porch steps.

"Look, Princess — it's Patches! Your old friend Patches from last summer!"

On the wide railing, fluffy and fat and sleepy, Princess was taking the first sunbath of the season. Lazily perking one pink, tufted ear at the sound of Mary Ellen's voice, she opened her eyes a mere crack — then leaped wildly to her feet as Minerva was suddenly plopped down in front of her. Not knowing her old friend at first, just seeing that there was another cat on *her* railing, she backed swiftly away, hissing. Her long, white fur stood straight up on her back as she stared into Minerva's wide, green eyes, and all at once Minerva was hissing too.

"Hey, come on now, you two! You're *friends*, remember?"

Mary Ellen was hovering worriedly over the two of them, patting them both, dragging them together, saying their names over and over. Suddenly Princess and Minerva were nose to nose, sniffing, quivering — remembering. Hisses turned into cautious meows, Princess's fur settled back into place, and all in one pleased moment, they knew each other for sure.

Within minutes, a huge saucer of milk appeared on the porch floor, and as Mary Ellen and her surprised parents stood watching, Minerva and Princess were contentedly drinking together as though they had never been apart at all.

It was good, Minerva thought happily, to have them all back again. There would be milk every day now, there would be heaping dishes of Tastee Tidbits, there would be cozy fires on chilly nights — oh, yes, it was good to have them back. She was still her own independent self, of course, but now and then she liked a taste of the housecat life. Now and then — and only for as long as she chose.

Later, when the family had gone down to the beach, Minerva and Princess stretched companionably out on the porch railing, drowsily licking their whiskers, washing their faces.

"You're looking well," remarked Princess. "How was the winter?"

"Oh, the usual," said Minerva. "A couple of snowstorms. A visit or two from my shiftless husband. A batch of kittens. Nothing much."

"Was it a hard winter?"

"No worse than ever. The bad weather bothered my gimpy leg a bit — but I managed."

"Old place looks about the same," said Princess, squinting out over the sparkling bay, "and, oh, how good it feels to be out in the open air again."

"It must," said Minerva, "after being cooped up indoors all winter long. I don't know how you stand it. Never a walk on a sunny day, never a climb up a tree, never a good mouse hunt — "

"Oh, they let me out *this* year," Princess said proudly, "any time I wanted to go. After that long winter I spent here with you, living off the land and managing to keep myself alive, they knew I could take care of myself. They don't pack me up in cat cases anymore, either."

"Really?" said Minerva. "No cat shows this year?"

"Only one — but I didn't win a thing. Not even an Honorable Mention."

"Why not? Did you do something wrong?"

"Yes," said Princess, with an amused twitch of her whiskers. "What I did was — I bit the judge."

"You did?" Minerva was astounded. "A well-behaved show cat like you? Why on earth would you do a thing like that?"

"I didn't like him fooling with my teeth, that's why. What they do is, they pry each cat's mouth open, and then they take a long look at each and every tooth. Didn't used to mind it much — but this time, suddenly I didn't see any sense to being annoyed for no better reason than having my teeth looked at. So I gave him a good nip, right in the thumb. Poor fellow let out a yelp and dropped me like a hot potato. That was the end of my career as a show cat."

"Good for you," said Minerva. "That sort of thing must be a terrible bother. It's always nice to be admired — but if you ask *me*, parading around in a ring, and then having your mouth poked open by a stranger is too much of a price to pay."

"Yes," said Princess, "and anyhow, my *family* admires me. That's all that matters."

"I suppose so," said Minerva, looking out over the beach, spotting the familiar flowered umbrella that shielded Princess's family from the hot sun, "and sometimes I think they're rather fond of me too — gimpy leg and all."

"You know they are," said Princess. "They wanted to take you home last year, remember?"

"I remember," Minerva said (rather wistfully, Princess thought), "but you know me. Never was a one to settle down and belong to somebody. I'm free as the air, and that's the way I like it. I come and go as I please, I do what I like, I set up housekeeping wherever I choose — ah, yes, my dear — the independent life, that's the life for old Minerva. Peace, quiet, not a worry in the world . . ."

The sound of her words was as soft and rhythmic as the breaking of waves on the shore, and before long they felt themselves drowsing, dozing in the warm summer sun. Dreaming of Tastee Tidbits and pattings and saucers of sweet, rich milk, Minerva couldn't help remembering that there was a whole lot to be said for the cozy housecat life too. It just might be nice to try it again — for a while, at least.

★ ★ ★

On bright, warm days, Princess and Minerva scouted the fields for mice, roamed the beach in search of popped-open clams and mussels, snoozed away the afternoons in the cool darkness underneath the boardwalk. It was just like old times — except for the evenings. The very minute the blue shadows of dusk began falling over the boardwalk, Princess dashed for the safety of her own front porch and meowed to be let in for the night.

"I never want to be lost again," she told Minerva, "and get left behind by mistake. At night — *indoors* is the place to be."

"Suit yourself," Minerva would say, "but *outdoors* is the place for me — unless it happens to be raining. I just might get in the mood for a moonlight stroll, and no one would trouble to let me out in the middle of the night. I'll just curl up here on the porch swing."

She rarely entered her old home at all anymore, now that the porch furniture was in place. The squeaky old swing was far more comfortable than the damp pile of rags underneath the house, and it was lots easier just to scamper down the steps when she was in the mood for a walk than it was to slither out underneath the splintery trelliswork below.

Besides that, she could watch the moonlight sparkling on the water, and lull herself to sleep with the gentle sound of waves lapping at the shore.

On a night when the moon was full, casting a glittering path of orange across the bay, Minerva found herself unable to close an eye. It was far too magnificent a night, she decided, for mere sleep, and at once she was off down the steps. It was a perfect night for mousing — she'd be able to spot the silly creatures plain as day — and she headed directly for the open fields that lay across the back road.

An annoying car or two, blinding her with their bright headlights, zipped past, and Minerva waited patiently until they were out of sight. Her old, gimpy leg — the one she'd injured in that awful blizzard two winters ago — sometimes gave out on her, and even when it didn't, she just wasn't as swift as she used to be. No point in taking foolish chances.

Staring up and down the moonlit road, she saw no lights in either direction, and in a quick, lopsided bound, she was across the road and pouncing happily through the long grass. What a shame Princess hadn't come along! There was nothing, Minerva thought, more amusing than a moonlight mouse hunt — and tonight there seemed to be dozens of little field mice zigzagging mindlessly through the grass. She wasn't a bit hungry, of course (there had been shrimp-flavored Tastee Tidbits for supper), but the pouncing was great sport, and there wasn't a single mouse she had her eye on that she didn't catch. There were hopping toads too, and before long Minerva had pounced herself into exhaustion. Now, she decided breathlessly, *now* she would go home and sleep.

But she'd come a long way, and since she happened to be out on a mouse hunt, it seemed silly just to walk home without trying to catch anything along the way. And so she pounced. And pounced again. And — oh! What was that? Could she be so lucky? Yes! It was a scared little rabbit, bounding crazily along just in front of her! What fun it would be to pounce on it, tease it a bit, then let it go. She wasn't, of course, as fast as she used to be — hadn't, in fact, caught a rabbit in months —but it would be worth a try. Just for the sport.

But the rabbit streaked in all directions, hiding itself in clumps of tall grass, springing out again, bounding madly over the fields, then turning and running another way altogether. It was a real challenge, and though Minerva didn't think she had a chance in the world of catching it, she hated to give up without a really good chase. Certainly she had the creature scared out of whatever wits it had — maybe it would turn senselessly around and run in *her* direction. She'd just keep her eyes fastened on it, and then —

Suddenly, not paying attention to anything but the rabbit, Minerva was aware of blinding lights — lights coming straight at her — and all at once she knew she'd dashed foolishly out into the road! With a mighty bound she leaped for the other side, and — in just that short, terrifying instant — the gimpy hind leg collapsed beneath her as limply as a blade of grass in a hard rain. She felt a huge bump, felt herself flying through the air, felt the blinding light searing her eyes. She felt her body abruptly thudding into a tangle of scratchy weeds.

And then — all at once — she felt nothing at all.

Danny

She awoke to a strange, humming sound, to the babble of human voices, to darkness all around. Struggling to move her aching body, Minerva discovered that the floor beneath her was vibrating, that the humming sound was coming from down below. Overhead she could feel a warm wind rushing at her, ruffling her fur, and at once she saw an open window. Outside, the orange moon seemed to be sailing along in the sky — and yet never out of sight, always there. Dark trees were also whisking past the window, and all in one astonished moment, Minerva knew where she was.

Never in all her life had she been inside a car, and though Princess had told her there was nothing at all unpleasant about an automobile ride, the very fact of being closed *in*, not out in the open air where she belonged, filled her with a sudden panic. She would make a leap for the open window, she decided at once, and then — if the car wasn't moving too fast — she would jump down into the darkness and get herself home.

But as she gathered her four feet beneath her, a searing pain shot up her gimpy hind leg, and at once she felt herself collapsing into an anguished heap on the floor. Her whole body was throbbing with pain, and as she tried to roll over on her side, tried to ease the pressure on her leg, she couldn't help crying out her misery. Suddenly a hand was sliding timidly down her side, smoothing her fur.

"She's coming out of it, Mom. Her eyes are open now, and she's kind of wiggling around. Maybe she's okay."

Looking up, Minerva saw that the voice and the gentle hand belonged to a solemn, worried looking little boy — a boy she had never seen before. The voice from the front seat was strange too, a woman's voice.

"Poor thing. Just don't touch her, Danny. You never know what bones might be broken."

At once the small hand was gone, but the boy's face was still close as he bent to study Minerva.

"She hurts all over, I think. But mostly it's

that back leg. It's stretched out in kind of a funny, twisty way. Is that what's broken, do you think?"

"Might be." This time the voice from the front seat belonged to a man. "But, oh, I hope not. I feel just awful. I've never hit an animal before. If only we hadn't got ourselves lost out there on the highway, we'd have been here long before dark, and then — "

"It wasn't your fault, Daddy. You couldn't see her — and she just came so *fast*."

"Maybe it's just bumps and bruises."

The woman's voice sounded all quavery, and Minerva could tell that she felt awful too. "Maybe nothing at all is broken. We'll just find a veterinarian in the village first thing in the morning, and I'm sure he'll be able to fix her up."

"When she's all well again, can we keep her, Mom?"

"Oh, no. I'm sure she belongs to somebody, a nice calico like that. We'll just make inquiries along the boardwalk, and we'll ask the veterinarian. This is such a tiny place — somebody's bound to know where she belongs."

"What if nobody does? Then can we keep her?"

"No, Danny, we can't. You know Grandma's

allergic to cats — they make her all sneezy —
and we'll be spending the whole summer with
Grandma. We definitely can't keep a cat. But if
we don't find out who owns her, we'll see that
she gets herself a good home somewhere, I
promise. And in the meantime, I'm sure
Grandma won't mind taking her in for the
night. We'll just find a nice box — "

Box! Minerva's ears perked at the sound of
the terrible word, and her eyes were wide
with fear. They were going to pack her up in
a dark box — and then they were going to take
her to a veterinarian! That was another word
she knew — Princess had told her all about
veterinarians and what they did to sick cats.
They poked them with needles, she remembered, and they stuffed nasty pills down their
throats, and sometimes they wrapped them up
in bandages so that they could barely move.
They even kept them in cages!

Well, she'd fool them all, that's what she'd
do. She'd get herself out of that box some way,
no matter how much it hurt to move so much
as a muscle, and then she'd find her way to the
boardwalk — and home. Mary Ellen would
take care of whatever was wrong with her, she
was sure of it — and Mary Ellen would know

enough not to cart her off to a veterinarian. Minerva had healed herself many times, just by patience and lots of licking, and she could certainly do it again. No boxes for old Minerva, she decided firmly, and no veterinarians, either!

But when the car crunched into the driveway of Grandma's house, and the humming sound stopped, Minerva was dismayed to find that she couldn't get herself even as far as the open door! Every tiny movement brought a stab of pain, and that silly leg of hers dragged along the floor as limply and uselessly as her bedraggled tail.

Another voice joined the others just outside the door, and in a moment she found herself staring into a bright, bobbing light.

"Poor creature," said the new voice," — AtCHOO! — poor, poor puss. There's a box up on the porch, Danny — atCHOO! — and you can take a towel off the line to pick her up in. And then we'll just — atCHOO! — take her inside where it's warm."

"Careful now," said Daddy, and before Minerva could do more than let out a yowl of pain and outrage, she found herself sliding helplessly across the floor on a towel, being gently wrapped in it, then lowered into a cardboard grocery carton. Not an inch of her body didn't ache, and Minerva had never felt so exhausted in all her life. No question about it, she would have to put off her escape until she got at least a little of her strength back. A good night's sleep, she decided, would have her up and out of this silly box by morning.

As they carried her slowly up the porch steps, Minerva was relieved to discover — briefly sniffing the air — that she could smell not only the sea, but the salty, familiar old planks of the boardwalk that ran the length of the beach. She was not far from home, then. She'd get herself an early start in the morning, long before anyone was up, and in no time at all she'd be climbing her own porch steps.

In the meantime, the people hovering over the box, talking in hushed, worried voices, were kind, wouldn't be a whole lot of bother. And after all, she reasoned wearily, one night in a box wasn't the worst thing in the world that would ever happen to her.

Gratefully, ignoring the tiny saucer of milk Danny insisted on setting down in the corner of the box, Minerva eased her throbbing limbs into as comfortable a position as she could manage, closed her eyes, and dozed.

The Steel Table

But it was not a good sleep. Glaring, remembered lights flashed on and off in Minerva's head, and the car motor still seemed to be humming beneath her. Even the babble of strange, worried voices lingered in the darkness of the unknown kitchen. Her gimpy leg throbbed unmercifully, jolting her awake with the slightest movement, and there was no way she could reach any of her aches and pains with her healing tongue. All she could manage was a fitful doze now and then, and when the first thin rays of morning sun slanted across the floor, she was wide awake.

"Hi there, Puss. How ya doing?" Suddenly Danny's round, freckled face was peering down at her. "Hey, you didn't even drink your milk. Aren't you hungry? Here, Puss, let me get it a little closer."

Minerva had forgotten all about the milk, didn't really want it, but decided sensibly that it might give her a bit of strength. Pulling herself up just enough to lap feebly at the saucer Danny had set under her nose, she found herself too weak to hold her head up for long, and soon she was as drenched around the whiskers as a sloppy kitten. But she drank, and it tasted good.

"There. Isn't that better?" Danny was beaming. "Hey, Grandma, come look. She drank every bit of her milk."

"AtCHOO! That's wonderful, Danny. Maybe she's not so badly hurt after all. They say a really sick animal never wants food."

"Maybe she's just bruised and banged up, the way Mom said. Maybe there's nothing busted, not even that funny leg. Can you tell just by looking, Grandma?"

"Well, I can't really come too close, Danny, because — atCHOO! — because — "

"She's even washing herself. She must feel okay after all. Maybe we should take her out of the box and see if she can walk."

To her own surprise, Minerva discovered that she very definitely did *not* want to be taken out of the box. Though Danny's hands were gentle, she yowled the very instant they touched her, clawing wildly at the towel beneath her. She wanted to lie here until she was well, and she hoped they'd have the good sense just to leave her alone. A few days of peace and quiet, a bit of licking when she could manage it, some good food now and then, and she'd be good as new. She'd recovered from other injuries as bad as this — often — and she could do it again.

The boy snatched his hands back out of the box, then timidly stretched one out to pat her gently on the top of her head.

"It's okay, Puss. You don't have to come out if you don't want to."

Good. They *were* going to leave her alone then. Before long she heard the clatter of breakfast dishes, the hum of voices, and in a moment Danny's hand was gone and no faces were looking down at her. The milk had made her drowsy, and as the morning sun grew warmer on her back, she felt herself drifting into a truly restful sleep. She was going to be fine.

But before the sun was high in the sky, the box was suddenly moving, there was the bang of a door, and all at once the humming of the car motor. They were not going to leave her alone after all! Her ears perked fearfully each time the car slowed down, and she knew that if they didn't find Mary Ellen and her family, she'd be carted off to the veterinarian! She could hear Danny and his father calling out to people all along the road — and she could hear strange voices saying that they didn't know anybody who owned a calico. She even heard one man, peering down at her through the car window, remark that she was "an ugly old bag of bones," and that she must surely be a stray.

Highly insulted as she was, Minerva reflected that being a "stray" was perfectly fine with her (though she preferred to call herself "an independent cat"), and all she wanted was to be on her own again. But as she moved about in the box, struggling to stand up, she knew it was going to be a long, long time before she could run away. Right now she couldn't even *walk*!

The veterinarian was kind, but Minerva hissed at him just the same, telling him that she needed no help, thank you, and would manage quite nicely on her own. But he had a good grip on all four of her feet, and there was no way she could take a swat at him, or even a nip. Holding her firmly down on a cold steel table, he was running his thumb up and down her gimpy leg, talking all the while — not to her, but to Danny and his father — in a quiet voice.

"It's a break, all right, but not a very bad one. And I think this cat was already lame before you hit her. The leg has definitely been broken before, and I don't think it was ever set properly — if at all."

"Can you fix it?" Danny wanted to know. "Can you get it back the way it was?"

"Not the way it was before it was ever broken," said the veterinarian, "but I can heal the new break. The poor thing will always have a limp — but ten days or so in a cast, and she'll be feeling fine. Just leave her with me, and I'll call you when it's time to take her home."

"The sad thing is," Daddy said, "I don't think she *has* a home. We inquired all along the boardwalk, and nobody seemed to know a thing about her. She's a stray, most likely. *We* can't keep her, I'm sorry to say, and —"

"Are you sure, Daddy? Are you sure we can't keep her?"

"I'm sure, Son. This cat — or any cat — wouldn't be good for Grandma. But maybe the doctor can find her a home. Do you think that's possible, Doctor?"

"It won't be easy." The doctor looked sorrowfully down at Minerva. "I mean, she's not exactly a kitten — and no beauty, either. But I'll try."

"Good," said Daddy. "And in the meantime, we'll make some more inquiries. We never did try the other end of the boardwalk, and if we don't find an owner — well, maybe somebody will take her in."

"I *hope* so," Danny said sadly, giving Minerva a final, tender pat. "She's a nice old puss. Oh, I hope she gets a good home!"

"I'll do everything possible," said the doctor, "just as soon as I've fixed up her leg and tended to all those bumps and bruises. If we're going to find her a home — well, she'll have to look a whole lot prettier than she does right now. Come on, Puss, we'll get right at it."

Before she knew what was happening, Minerva found herself being rolled over, wrapped in a towel so tightly that she couldn't move so much as a whisker. And then she was being carried into another room, stretched out on another steel table, and — with a suddenness that startled her out of her wits — rolled abruptly out of the towel and speared with a long, sharp needle. She heard herself yowling in pain, she heard the doctor's voice saying "easy now, Puss," and then she heard nothing at all. The feeling of cold steel beneath her was suddenly gone, and all at once she seemed to be plunging through the air — down and down and down — into a cool, welcoming blackness.

Minerva Caged

It was the sound of dogs barking that brought her foggily awake, and for a long moment, blinking in the half-darkness, Minerva thought that she'd been snoozing underneath the boardwalk. She'd never heard quite so many dogs at once, and she hoped they weren't going to chase her. It would be a terrible nuisance, stiff and sore as she was, to have to dash across the beach and climb to the top of a rock . . .

And then she heard the sound of meowing somewhere, the whimpering of a puppy, the faint mew of tiny kittens. The sounds seemed to come from all around her — above, below, on either side — and in a startled flash Minerva was wide awake.

She was not lying on the cool sand underneath the boardwalk, she discovered at once, but inside some sort of strange box lined with shredded newspapers. Three sides of it were solid, and the top was closed — but just in front of her eyes there was a wall of wire mesh that she could see through.

A cage! Suddenly, remembering all that Princess had told her about visits to veterinarians, Minerva knew that she was inside a cage! She also knew that she was surrounded by other wretched animals in other cages — and that she was going to get herself out of this cramped, noisy place as quickly as possible!

But as she leaped for the wire mesh —knowing that it must surely be a door — a heavy weight on her gimpy leg dragged her suddenly backward, and she saw that the old familiar leg had turned into what seemed to be a great mass of white stone! It hurt to move it even slightly, and at the first stab of pain, Minerva let out a yowl of anguish.

"Better not move just yet, dear," came a calm, pleasant voice from the cage directly across from hers. "I had a broken leg once myself, and I found that just not moving was the best cure. Take your time."

Peering through the mesh, Minerva saw that the voice came from a sleepy yellow tabby with a front paw wrapped in a fat bandage.

"It's best not to make too much fuss," the tabby went on. "No point in wearing yourself to a frazzle, that's what I always say. They're not going to let you out anyway, until they're good and ready. You might as well settle down and make the best of it."

"Not *me*," said Minerva. "I'm an independent cat, that's what I am, and I have no intention of being kept in a cage like a silly canary. They'll let *me* out of here in no time, you can be sure of it. Just listen."

At once Minerva set up a yowl — a long, wailing yowl that was loud enough to drown out the barking of the dogs, loud enough to

STRAY-BROKEN LEG

make the yellow tabby put her paws over her ears and squinch her eyes shut.

"That should do it," said Minerva, pausing just long enough to take a good breath, "if I can just manage to keep it up. A nasty racket like that, and they'll want to be rid of me soon enough. And if that doesn't do it, I can always hiss and look mean. Nobody likes a mean cat."

But — to her great surprise — somebody did. Hiss and yowl as she would, nobody objected even slightly, and the human face that suddenly appeared outside the cage smiled tenderly in at her. It was not the doctor, but a lady in a white smock, and when she spoke, her voice was gentle and soft.

"Poor puss," she murmured sympathetically. "Does it hurt much? I'll just give you something to make you feel better."

The very instant the door was opened — only part way, but enough for a possible getaway — Minerva heaved herself forward, but managed to get no more than the tip of her nose through the opening. The lady's hands were upon her at once, holding her firmly down, patting her head, smoothing her fur.

"There now, Puss," she said calmly, "just hold still for a second. This won't hurt a bit, I promise."

Suddenly the lady gathered up a bit of loose skin just over Minerva's shoulder, then plunged one of those awful needles into it. She was right — it didn't hurt a bit — but Minerva yowled fiercely just the same, telling the lady quite plainly that she was not the sort of cat to stick needles into. All she needed, if they only knew, was a bit of peace and quiet — and privacy. If they'd just take that heavy white thing off her leg, she'd lick it well in no time, and after that she'd be on her way. A quiet day or two sunning on the porch railing would do her a whole lot more good than lying around in a dark cage being stuck full of holes!

To her amazement, Minerva suddenly heard her howls of outrage fading away into nothing more than faint, halfhearted meows, and in a moment she felt too lazy to bother with any sound at all. Nothing seemed to hurt anymore, and though she didn't feel sleepy, there was a pleasant tingling numbness in her bad leg that made her feel comfortable for the first time in days.

As the lady in the white smock firmly latched the door of her cage, Minerva knew that the yellow tabby had been quite right — they were not going to let her out, no matter how much fuss she kicked up, until they were good and ready. No point in wearing herself out, she decided sensibly, if all that howling and yowling wasn't going to do her any good.

But days and days went by, and no one ever opened the door far enough, or long enough, for her to slip out. The doctor came by a few times to look at her and poke her uncomfortably about, the lady in the white smock showed up to stuff huge white pills down her throat (patting her a bit to make up for the indignity), and a young man in jeans came in twice a day to thrust a dish of food into her cage and straighten things up.

A lady came to take the yellow tabby home, stopping in front of Minerva's cage just long enough to mutter "poor thing," and once, Danny and his father came in to see how she was getting along. But no one showed any signs of taking her out of the cage, and Minerva couldn't help wondering — with a feeling of panic — if she was going to spend her entire *life* here!

A day finally came when the doctor lifted her out of the cage — all the way out! — but to Minerva's dismay he did not set her free. Instead he took her back to that cold steel table where she'd been forced to lie on the day she arrived, not letting go for an instant. Fearful that another terrible needle might be plunged into her, Minerva set up a loud, outraged yowl.

But there was no needle. This time the doctor came at her with a long, shiny thing she'd never seen before, slashing swiftly into the heavy white stone that had been weighing down her gimpy leg. In a moment it was gone, lying in two neat pieces on the table, and her leg felt suddenly as light as a feather. Good! She was free to make a run for it now! At once Minerva made a lunge for the edge of the table.

But the silly leg immediately slid sideways on the slippery steel, collapsing beneath her, and before she could heave herself upright again, the doctor was dragging her back to the middle of the table.

"Easy there, Puss," he said. "You're not ready to do any jumping around just yet. A little walk from here to the door, that's all for today."

Setting her on the floor, the doctor watched as Minerva stood wavering uncertainly on her three good legs, then timidly tried out the gimpy one. It didn't work! It went all funny and weak every time she put her weight on it, and though it didn't hurt a bit, it wasn't the slightest bit useful, either!

Ah well, she thought grimly, at least she didn't have that heavy weight dragging her down in the back anymore — she'd just have to make do with three legs instead of four. A terrible nuisance, but certainly possible. Tucking the bad leg up underneath her, Minerva was off at once — at a wobbly, lopsided gallop — heading for the open door.

But the doctor was upon her at once, kicking the door shut with his foot, grasping her firmly around the middle. Then — for all the world as though she were a helpless kitten — he stood her up on her hind legs and *made* her walk on them.

"There you go, Puss. See? It works. Just a little weak, that's all. A little exercise now and then, and in a few days you'll be good as new. You won't have much of a limp, either. That'll help when we try to find you an owner."

Minerva's ears flattened at the very sound of the word, and her tail drooped in misery. They hadn't found Mary Ellen and her family, then — the only people in the world who knew that she wanted no owner, wanted only to be free! Danny and his father must have given up halfway down the boardwalk, or simply missed Mary Ellen's house. They must have decided, finally, that she was a lonely, homeless stray — and not an independent cat who liked her life that way.

But an owner, she supposed, was her only hope of escape, and as the doctor locked her firmly back into her cage, she settled gloomily down to wait for someone who might take a liking to her. Being owned, she decided, would be a far better thing than spending the rest of her life in a cage!

When people came to see her, she tried hard to be pleasant, to be a nice, calm, likable housecat. But almost everybody who stopped in front of her cage seemed to want a little kitten instead, seemed to find things wrong with her.

"Homely," sniffed one lady. "That's a homely cat if I ever saw one. But if you ever get a really *pretty* calico, let me know."

"Not that one," said a little girl. "The colors are wrong. Not enough yellow. I want one with a whole lot of yellow."

"Skinny," said a fat little boy, "much too skinny. I want one that's nice and plump and cuddlesome."

"She's got kind of a wild look," said a fluttery lady. "Just see how she's staring at me with those fierce-looking eyes. I always wanted a real calico — but not *that* one. She makes me nervous."

"Not enough fur," complained another little girl. "I want to name my cat Fluffy — and that one's not. Just look how short her hair is. You sure couldn't call *her* Fluffy."

"Nobody is ever going to want me," Minerva mourned over and over again, watching possible owners leave with adorable kittens and frisky puppies. "I'm just not cute, that's the thing. Let's face it, I'm a skinny old bag of bones with a limp, that's what I am — and who's ever going to want a skinny old bag of bones with a limp?"

"Patience," advised the plump, motherly looking black Persian who had moved into the tabby's cage, "just have a little patience. One of these days, someone will be absolutely crazy about you, mark my words." She narrowed her amber eyes and looked wise. "Just remember, my dear, not everybody has to like you. It only takes one."

And on the very next day — to Minerva's great surprise — the "one" came.

Mrs. Weatherington

The voice outside her cage sounded, at first, as though it belonged to a small, excited child. It was high and thin, and to Minerva's astonishment, the first words it spoke to her were "Pretty kitty! Oh, what a pretty kitty!" But the voice had a sort of quaver to it, and at once, peering through the mesh of her door, Minerva saw that it belonged to an old lady with a pleasant, smiling face.

"What a pretty kitty!" she said again, bending low to look in at Minerva. "Oh, yes, Doctor, she *does* look like my poor old Callie. The markings are very much the same, don't you agree? Of course, no cat in the world could ever replace my Callie, rest her soul, but this one could almost be her twin." The old lady sighed, then looked sadly away from Minerva. "I don't know whether I'm ready for another cat just yet, though. It hasn't been more than a few hours since my poor old Callie — oh, Doctor, I shouldn't have taken her on such a long trip, an old cat like that. I just know I shouldn't have!"

"She wouldn't have lasted much longer anyway," the doctor said reassuringly. "She was a very old cat. And she went peacefully."

"I know," said the old lady. "I'm so glad I happened through this village when her time came. You've been very kind, Doctor. But, oh, how I hate going home without her! We've been together for so many years . . ."

"It's hard," said the doctor, "but I really think another cat — especially one that looks so much like Callie — might be just the thing to cheer you up. And this one's in need of a good home, poor thing."

"I suppose you're right, Doctor. And I'd be doing a kindness, wouldn't I?" Once again she peered through the mesh door, studying Minerva. "Is she gentle and well-behaved?"

"Well" — the doctor didn't seem to know quite what to say " — to tell you the truth, Mrs. Weatherington, she hasn't the best disposition I've ever seen. But, of course, she's been through a difficult experience, I'm sure you understand that, and she's just a bit — uh — skittery. But a little kindness seems to work wonders. In time, I'm sure she'll settle down and make a fine pet."

"Is she quite well, Doctor?"

"Oh, yes. We've been exercising her every day, and almost all of the stiffness is gone. She'll always have a bit of a limp, I'm afraid — the result of an old injury — but she's feeling perfectly fine."

"Could she stand an hour's ride in a car, do you think? I'm on my way home, you know, and I wouldn't want to worry about her. Naturally I'd take her in Callie's old carrying case — but I've heard that some cats don't like being closed up."

"She's quite used to it," said the doctor. "She's been closed up in a cage for two weeks. I'm sure it won't bother her a bit."

But it did bother her a bit. In fact, it bothered her a whole lot — she was plain tired of being inside things! All the way to Mrs. Weatherington's home Minerva yowled, scratching at the sides of the case and racketing furiously around. From the front seat, Mrs. Weatherington's voice, chattering at her all the way, sounded strained and nervous, and once in a while Minerva felt the car wildly swerving from side to side.

Grateful as she was to the old lady, Minerva was determined to make a run for it the very moment the lid was raised, and when the car finally came to a jolting halt, she gathered herself into a crouch at the bottom of the case, ready to spring. Through the open door of the car, a warm, beautiful summer breeze drifted past the holes in her carrying case — the first whiff of the outdoors she'd had in *weeks* — and Minerva was wild to be free.

But to her dismay, she felt the case being hauled out of the car, then carried up a flight of steps, then set abruptly down — with the lid still firmly closed! There was the sound of a key in a lock, a door squeaked open, and then she was suddenly lifted up once more, then plunked down again. Two loud bangs told her that the door — and then another door — had been closed behind her.

"There you are, Kitty. We're home, safe and sound. You may come out now."

Suddenly there was dazzling sunshine all around — and with a loud, joyful meow, Minerva leaped over the edge of the carrying case and up to the highest, airiest place she could find. Pots of geraniums lined the sill of the newly opened window, but Minerva squeezed herself among them, pressing her nose to the screen. The light summer breeze washed delightfully over her, and the sun she had not seen in so many long, dark days warmed her fur. Outside there were tall trees, and a wide lawn of uncut grass. This was going to be a fine place to stay — at least long enough to get back enough strength for the journey home — and at once Minerva meowed to be let out.

"Oh, no, no, no, Kitty. You may sit on the windowsill any time you choose, but you may not go out. I have never believed that pets should be allowed to roam about outdoors. My Callie went out only when I took her on a leash — and, oh, how she did enjoy a nice walk around the block. You just settle down now, Kitty, and maybe in a day or two, when you're used to things, I'll unpack Callie's old leash and collar, and you and I can go for a walk together. Won't that be fun? In the meantime, I'm just going to keep you here in the kitchen. Be a good kitty, now, and I'll fix you up a nice litter box."

All at once Minerva was alone, pushing helplessly at the screen, yearning for the feel of the green grass against her fur, the roughness of the tree trunks beneath her weakened claws. Leaping from the windowsill, she paced the tiny kitchen, moving from one corner to another, looking for another way out. But the back door was firmly shut, and so was the door that led from the kitchen into the rest of the house. There was no way out at all!

Jumping back to the windowsill and cramming herself uncomfortably in among the geraniums, Minerva suddenly realized that somehow she had exchanged one cage for another!

When Mrs. Weatherington came back — hastily slamming the door behind her — she brought with her not only a litter box, but a huge wicker basket with a plump mattress in it.

"Just see what I've brought for you," she said, setting it underneath the kitchen table. "It's Callie's old bed. Won't that be a fine place to sleep? Come try it, Kitty!"

But Minerva had no intention of trying out Callie's old bed. She wanted to sleep *outdoors*, not in any silly wicker basket, and she

would just stay on the windowsill until Mrs. Weatherington understood. Firmly bunching herself up into a ball, Minerva sat motionless, glaring. Even the saucer of milk that suddenly appeared on the floor just below the windowsill did not bring her down, and it was plain to Minerva that Mrs. Weatherington — fluttery and upset — hadn't the faintest idea what to do about her.

"You're not like my Callie at all," she kept saying sadly, "even though you do look like her. Callie was so cuddlesome and affectionate, and she always came when I called her. I don't understand you, Kitty, I really don't. I should think you'd be glad to have such a good home!"

For a moment Minerva considered coming down and being nice to Mrs. Weatherington. The poor lady was trying so hard to please her — and after all, this bright, sunny kitchen was a far better place to be than the dark old cage that had been her home for the past few weeks. Perhaps, when Mrs. Weatherington got to know her better, she'd stop mourning for old Callie, and understand that Minerva was an entirely different sort of cat — an independent cat with a need to come and go as she chose.

Though she knew that she was never in this world going to be "cuddlesome and affectionate," like Callie, Minerva could be a perfectly respectable housecat when she wanted to be — and suddenly she wanted to be. A day or two of rest and nourishment, she thought sensibly, would be just the thing to put some meat on her bones, build up her flabby muscles. It was, after all, going to be a long walk home.

It was the sound of the electric can opener — and then the delicious smell of Tastee Tidbits in the air — that finally brought Minerva down, determined to be as decent a housecat as she could manage. Taking the time to rub gratefully up against Mrs. Weatherington's ankle, she dove at once into the best and biggest meal she'd had in weeks.

From the start, Mrs. Weatherington was good to her. Within a day, Minerva was allowed out of the kitchen, allowed to prowl about the rest of the house wherever and whenever she wished. She could sleep on any piece of furniture that happened to take her fancy, she was welcome in every room — and Mrs. Weatherington even moved all the geraniums to the kitchen table so that Minerva could stretch herself full length on the windowsill.

The food was a marvel. Though Minerva would have been more than satisfied with plain old canned cat food, and maybe a saucer of milk now and then, Mrs. Weatherington insisted on *cooking* for her, producing such unheard of delicacies as salmon with buttered bread crumbs, warm, frothy mixtures of egg and milk, and nicely broiled fresh mackerel.

In return for all this, Minerva purred frequently, rubbed up against Mrs. Weatherington's ankles before and after every meal, even jumped up into her lap on an occasional evening. She was, she thought, a truly model housecat — until the day Mrs. Weatherington came hopefully at her with Callie's old collar and leash.

"How about a nice little walk?" she suggested brightly. "I'll just fasten this collar around your — "

In a flash, Minerva had skittered under the sofa and backed herself against the wall. Never in all her independent life had she worn a scratchy collar around her neck — and the thought of parading about at the end of a leash was too ridiculous even to consider. No collar for old Minerva, and no leash either! More than anything, she wanted to be outdoors again — but she was *not* going to be tugged about like a silly, prancing poodle!

Within minutes, Mrs. Weatherington had put away the collar and leash, sorrowfully shaking her head and reminiscing about all those lovely walks she'd had with old Callie.

Hopefully Minerva came out from under the sofa, then scampered to the front door, meowing a pleading "meow!" But Mrs. Weatherington, not understanding, was upon her at once, swooping her abruptly up into her arms, carrying her into the kitchen.

"There," she said, plunking Minerva into the litter box beside the back door, "there you are, Kitty. Is that what you want?"

No! Leaping out of the box and over the kitchen table to the windowsill, Minerva clawed wildly at the screen, telling Mrs. Weatherington that she'd had enough of boxes, that all she wanted was to be *out*! She wanted to walk on the green grass, to sharpen her claws on a tree trunk — not that silly, falling-over scratching post Mrs. Weatherington had provided for Callie — to roll deliciously about, scratching her back, in the stony driveway. She might well come back for supper — yes, she probably would — but in the meantime, she wanted to be *free*!

"You might as well stop that scratching, Kitty," scolded Mrs. Weatherington. "You're only ruining the screen — and you know full well that no cat of mine is going to run about outdoors. Now just come down from there, and I'll give you a brand new catnip mouse to play with. And then — you know what? I'm going to think of a nice name for you. It's high time you had a name of your very own."

But Minerva did not want a brand new catnip mouse, nor did she want any name other than the one she already had, given to her by a long-forgotten family, way back when she'd been a tiny kitten — Minerva. As a matter of fact, plain old "Kitty" suited her just fine. Like "Puss," it was a name for a cat that didn't belong to anyone, and despite all the lounging around she'd done in the past few weeks, Minerva knew full well that she was never going to belong to Mrs. Weatherington — or anybody else.

Mrs. Weatherington didn't know it, though, and as the days went by, she seemed to feel that Minerva was settling down nicely. She no longer clawed at the window screens (no point in risking a broken claw, Minerva felt, if it wasn't going to get her anywhere), nor did she meow forlornly at the front or back door. All *that* ever brought was the immediate sight of that awful collar and leash, dangling from Mrs. Weatherington's hand, and the eager suggestion that she put it on now and "come for a walk, like a good kitty."

There was nothing to do, Minerva decided, but to behave like a proper housecat — and keep herself alert at all times for a possible means of escape.

Escape

Minerva behaved herself so well that sometimes Mrs. Weatherington was a bit careless about keeping doors shut. Once, on a morning when she stood chatting with the milkman, Minerva actually managed to slip out — but before she was halfway down the walk, Mrs. Weatherington had snatched her up, hanging firmly on to her until the milkman was gone and the door shut behind him.

"Bad girl!" she scolded Minerva. "Bad, bad Kitty. You know I don't allow you to go prowling about the neighborhood. Now you just stay inside, where you belong."

Mrs. Weatherington immediately became more watchful, and it was a long, long time before another door stood ajar for even a second. This time it happened at night, when a neighbor came to the front door to return something she had borrowed from Mrs. Weatherington. To Minerva's delight, the neighbor had no time to stop in for a visit, and so the two stood talking in the open doorway. Perfect! If she could just manage to streak out fast enough, thought Minerva, excitedly lashing her tail, she could lose herself in the darkness in no time!

Swiftly, leaping down from the living room windowsill where she'd been enjoying the cool night air, Minerva made a dash for the doorway, zipped through it, and was careening wildly about the dark front yard before Mrs. Weatherington could do more than make a useless grab for Minerva's disappearing tail.

"Come back, Kitty, come back, come back!"

But Minerva had no intention of coming back — ever. Fond as she was of Mrs. Weatherington, she knew that the tiny, closed-up house she lived in was definitely not the place for old, independent Minerva. The place for Minerva was out here in the cool darkness, out here where there were no walls, and only the wide, starry sky for a ceiling.

Diving through a hedge into the next yard, Minerva did not stop to enjoy the feeling of the fresh breeze ruffling her fur, did not stop to sniff the delicious damp grass, to glance even briefly at the great open sky overhead. For as long as she heard Mrs. Weatherington's frantic voice calling into the darkness, Minerva kept on running. She gave no thought to direction, only to the incredible thought that she was *free* — really free!

When the voice finally faded away, Minerva slowed down to as brisk a walk as she could manage with her still gimpy leg. Her sides were heaving, her tongue lolling from her mouth, and she realized that she was far from fit. All those weeks of doing nothing but eating and sleeping had made her muscles go slack, and Minerva knew at once that she'd need a night's rest before she could begin the journey home.

Home . . .

Stopping under a drooping mulberry tree in the middle of a strange front yard, Minerva sat down and began to think about home. She thought about the sea, the soft, lapping of waves on the shore at night, the delectable crabs and mussels to be found among the rocks at low tide, the salty, splintery old boardwalk where she loved sharpening her claws and scratching her back. She thought about Princess, about Mary Ellen, about her own dark, private home underneath the weathered old cottage on the boardwalk. She thought about the wide porch railing where she and Princess drowsed away the sunny mornings, and she thought about the wide, grassy fields behind the house, the fields that were alive with tiny, tasty creatures to catch.

She had been gone a very long time, and as she sat remembering all that had happened to her since that awful night of her accident, Minerva knew that home was far, far away. She'd been driven here, there, and everywhere in strange cars, and there was no way of knowing where she was, or which direction to take. All she knew, trying to remember each and every detail of home, was that every morning the bright sun came up out of the sea — and that at night it sank down behind the fields. It would be sensible, she thought, to head for the morning sun.

But she had a long night to get through first, and she knew she'd have to keep herself hidden. Mrs. Weatherington might just have taken it into her head to drive up and down the road in her car, looking for her. Perhaps she'd even have the neighbors out, bobbing flashlights under trees and into bushes. So far, not a single car had gone by, and there was no sign of a flashlight — but Minerva was going to take no chances.

Padding quietly around a large, dark house, Minerva explored countless backyards, looking for a suitable place to spend the night, finally settling herself beneath the dark, sheltering leaves of a huge, drooping willow. There was a little pond just beside it where she could have a good drink of water — in the morning, when she'd feel more like bothering about it — and there was a soft, mossy place close to the trunk where she could be every bit as comfortable as she had been in Callie's old bed.

Curling herself into a contented ball, Minerva slept — and dreamed of the sea.

The first light of morning sun glimmered through leafy treetops, and Minerva set directly off toward the spot where it seemed the brightest. Despite the huge dinner she'd had the night before, she was starving hungry, and she knew that the long drink of water she'd had at the little pond wouldn't keep her filled up for long. She wasn't far enough from Mrs. Weatherington's house to risk rummaging in any of the garbage cans she saw sitting by various back doors, and the wide, neatly trimmed lawns that stretched before her were not at all the sort of place to find mice running about. She would have to wait, she decided, until she got herself into some woods or some fields.

But the trees became sparser as she moved from one front yard to the next, and the lawns in front of the houses suddenly seemed to be no more than tiny patches of green. The houses were crowded together now, and between them no grass grew at all. They were strange looking houses — tall and squarish, with a whole lot of windows — and Minerva saw that some of them were connected to each other, with no space between.

Dozens of cars were zipping along the road, some of them more enormous than she'd ever seen. They had long rows of windows on each side, and to Minerva's amazement, there were faces in every one of them. They moved along with a loud, nerve-jarring rumble, and a terrible smell came out of them. Sometimes they made a honking sound that was immediately answered by horns in all the other cars, and sometimes the drivers yelled angrily at each other. Minerva decided to stay as far away from them as she could.

Suddenly crowds of people were all about her, and Minerva found herself ducking in and out of doorways, dodging hurrying footsteps. There were dogs on leashes, there were dogs *not* on leashes, and everywhere there was noise and clatter. Somehow she'd found her uncertain way into a strange, terrifying place, and for a moment Minerva considered dashing back to the quiet backyard where she'd started, and then beginning again in a different direction.

But the sun shone in front of her, and she knew that it never came up any other way than out of the sea. If she wanted to get home, then this was the way she would have to go. Far away, somewhere beyond this dreadful, rackety place, lay the cool, placid waters of her own remembered bay, and as she watched the sun rising higher and higher into the sky, Minerva pictured it shining down over the old porch railing where she took her sunbaths. Right this minute, she thought wistfully, Princess was probably stretched out on it, licking her whiskers, settling her breakfast.

Suddenly reminded of her own fierce hunger, Minerva wondered how on earth she was going to feed herself in this crazy, bustling place. The only morsels of food she'd found so far had been a discarded ice cream cone, crushed and melting on the sidewalk, and a tiny, stale bit of candy that had fallen out of a trash basket. Certainly, with nothing but hard cement beneath her feet, there would be no mice, no toads, no hopping little creatures to catch, and for the first time in all her independent life, Minerva had no idea how she was going to get herself a square meal.

Here and there, food smells drifted out of open doorways, but no one offered her anything, and she couldn't bring herself to beg. Once, a hurrying man dropped a soggy, crumbled bit of a doughnut on the ground, and once she found a half-eaten apple lying in the gutter. Not her sort of food at all, she thought with a disgusted twitch of her nose, but it would tide her over until she found herself a wide open field somewhere.

But when the sun began to sink behind her, she was still walking on hard cement, and there were no fields in sight. There were fewer tall buildings now, but cars were still zipping along the road, people still hurrying in and out of doorways. Here and there a tiny, stunted tree peeked out from between two buildings, and Minerva was hopeful that soon she'd find a quiet green place to spend the night.

Keeping herself close to the buildings — she was very definitely not going to be hit by a car *again* — Minerva began to move at a run. Purple shadows were beginning to fall over the sidewalk, night was coming, and she had no intention of sleeping in a strange, dark doorway. With stray dogs still roaming the streets, she knew she wouldn't close an eye, and if she wanted to make any distance tomorrow, she'd need a good night's rest.

To her dismay, Minerva suddenly found that her still weak, gimpy old leg was beginning to give out on her, and that she couldn't run anymore. Slowing down to a tired limp, she knew that she was going to need a resting place soon — and that she was not going to make it all the way out to where a peaceful green field might be. Perhaps she could stop — for a while at least — in a nook between two buildings, or on a nice, safe window ledge. Sensibly, Minerva sat down and began to study the fronts of the buildings.

Suddenly a door opened behind her, light was spilling over the sidewalk, and a man in an apron was looking down at her.

"Hi there, Puss," he said in a pleasant voice.

"Where did you come from?" To Minerva's surprise, he bent down and patted her. "Skinny old thing, aren't you? Bet you haven't eaten all day. Am I right?"

Before she knew what was happening, Minerva was being picked up, then carried inside the lighted building. What now? What on earth did the man want with her? Was it possible that he was going to feed her? And if so, why couldn't he simply have set a dish of something or other outside the door?

Wildly, squirming in the man's arms, Minerva looked about, ready to break away and flee if there were any dogs or other dangers about. But there were no dangers, the place smelled of food, and the man seemed kind.

"There you are, Puss," he said, setting her gently on the floor and whisking the door shut with his foot, "go to it."

Go to *what*? Except for shelves and shelves of closed cans and boxes, a bin of vegetables, and a glass-fronted cabinet full of milk and eggs, there was no food in sight. The only thing Minerva could think to do was look questioningly up at the man and meow helplessly.

"Go to it, Puss," he said again. "There are

mice all over the place. They're into everything, and they're driving me out of my wits. What I need is a good mouser. Go to it."

Minerva couldn't believe her great good luck. Not only was she going to have a safe place to sleep all night, but she was going to have a feast of mice as well!

Before the man had even taken off his apron and turned out the light, Minerva was eagerly sniffing the air. She hadn't had a good hunt since the night of her accident, and though she'd have preferred pouncing about through a field of grass, she was more than willing to make do with an indoor hunt. She was hungry!

A tiny sound of scrabbling feet came to her perked-up ears, and by the time the man had stepped out into the dusky evening and locked the door shut behind him, Minerva was wriggling her way among stacks of boxes, stalking her first mouse.

Minerva and the Mice

"You're a marvel, Puss!" In the first bright light of morning, the man in the apron stood beaming down at Minerva, who was coming sleepily awake on the pile of paper bags where she'd spent the night. "Three of the nasty creatures in the storeroom alone, another two behind the counter — and no telling how many you had for supper. You're some dandy mouser, I'll say that!"

For a moment, drowsily stretching herself, Minerva forgot about the long journey ahead, and simply lay enjoying the feel of the man's large hand patting her head, tickling her pleasantly behind the ears.

"How about a little milk for your pains?" At once the man was rummaging around behind the counter, fishing out a discarded jar lid, then pouring milk into it and setting it on the floor. "Sorry it's so small, Puss, but if I give you any more than that, you won't do your job."

It *was* small, but Minerva licked it up gratefully. Despite the plump mouse she had devoured last night, she was remarkably hungry again, and she knew that today's journey was going to be long and hard. She needed every bit of nourishment she could get.

Taking only enough time to lick her whiskers clean, not even bothering to wash her face, Minerva walked immediately to the door and meowed to be let out. Through the glass door she could see that it was going to be a glorious, sunny day, and she was eager to be off.

But to her amazement, the man did not let her out.

"Oh, no, Puss," he said, swooping suddenly down upon her and picking her up, "you're not going anywhere. A good mouser like you isn't easy to come by, and the job is by no means finished. It's into the storeroom for you, Puss!"

It was a dark, cluttered room with huge piles of boxes all around, and only one tiny, dusty window. Scratching at the closed door, Minerva yowled furiously, but the man did nothing more than call cheerfully in to her, instructing her once again to "go to it."

For a long time, prowling helplessly from corner to corner, Minerva completely ignored the scrabbling little mice that seemed to be everywhere. Hungry as she was, the thought of food wasn't in her mind at all. The sun outside the tiny window was rising higher and higher into the sky, the day was passing, and Minerva could think of nothing but escape.

But when the man finally opened the door and came into the storeroom, he held her firmly back with his foot while he slammed the door behind him. Then he picked up a stack of cartons, did the same thing with his foot, and swiftly whisked the door shut in Minerva's face. Through the long, long day it happened many times — and not once did Minerva manage to dodge the huge foot.

When night came, she had demolished a mouse or two, but still felt hungry. The man gave her no more than another jar lid full of milk, and though he opened the door and allowed her into the other room, he had the front door closed and locked behind him before Minerva could make a dash for it.

There was nothing to do, she thought, staring sorrowfully into the quiet darkness, but feed herself as best she could — and hope that some day the man might be careless enough to leave the storeroom door ajar. She'd heard the tramping of feet in and out all day long, and she knew that if she could just manage to slip out of the storeroom, it would be a simple matter to race out through the open front door.

But days went by, nights went by, and never once was there a chance of escape. Minerva lived on a diet of mice, an occasional crunchy cockroach, milk, and whatever scraps the man chose to give her. Mornings and evenings he patted her, talked to her, praised her for the number of mice she was doing away with — but never did he consider setting her free.

"Best mouser I ever saw," he told her over and over again. "I don't know what I'd do without you, Puss. You just keep up the good work and you can live here forever."

Suddenly a crazy thought came into Minerva's head. Clearly the man was fond of her — but would he be just as fond if she didn't catch any mice? Would he bother keeping her just as a pet? She didn't think so. Pets lived in homes, not grocery stores — and pets were properly fed every day, not forced to hunt for a living. What this man needed, plain and simple, was a *mouse*cat, not a housecat!

At once Minerva knew what to do — or rather, what *not* to do. It was not going to be easy, keeping herself fit with no more food than tiny jar lids of milk and an occasional scrap, but if she could just manage to get through a day or two, she was sure the man would be more than ready to let her go.

She was right. Finding no dead mice about on the next few days, the man was at first puzzled, then annoyed, then angry.

"They've gotten into the crackers," he complained to Minerva, "and there are great big holes in that carton of imported cheese. If you don't get after them pretty soon, I'm just going to have to throw you out of here and get myself an exterminator. And I don't want to do that, because exterminators are expensive. Now you just get to work, Puss, or there'll be no milk for you tonight!"

Fortunately, the man was not at all the sort who would allow even a useless cat to starve to death, but it was plain that he was disappointed in Minerva.

"I thought I had myself a real mouser," he muttered one morning, grumpily pouring Minerva's milk into the lid, "but I guess even the best of them get lazy. From here in, Puss, you're on your own. You can stay here if you like — you're rather a nice old thing — or you can go. Suit yourself."

Minerva made short work of her tiny breakfast, and the very instant the man opened the front door for the day, she was through it like a streak. For a moment she stood blinking in the bright morning sun, not remembering at first which way she was heading.

The man made no move to snatch her back.

"So long, old Puss," he said (rather sadly, Minerva thought). "You're a smart old puss, you know that?"

Standing still just long enough to allow the man one final pat, Minerva pointed herself toward the rising sun and was briskly on her way.

By the time the evening shadows fell, they were dappling the ground with a pattern of leaves. Tall trees lined the road now, and there were no other buildings than a scattering of houses here and there. Once again there were wide lawns — not as neat as the ones around Mrs. Weatherington's house — and the grass felt good under Minerva's tired feet. There were even bushes and hedges to rest under when she felt like it, and Minerva knew that she was coming closer and closer to home.

There was no whiff of sea in the air, but the

little pine trees that thrust themselves up on the hillsides had the same stunted look as the pines along the seashore, and the earth underfoot had a grainy feel to it, like sand. Before long the grassy lawns turned brownish and stubbly — like the patchy little lawns that grew in the backyards of the boardwalk houses — and the air had a special freshness to it that she had not felt in a long time.

Field mice were everywhere for the taking, and by the time she curled up for the night, under a familiar sort of berry bush at the side of the road, Minerva wasn't a bit hungry. She could take care of herself quite nicely, she thought with satisfaction, without a single human being to help her (or get in her way!) — and, oh, how glorious it was to be her own independent self again!

Home

A day came when the first unmistakable tang of salt was in the air. Suddenly Minerva could see distant flocks of seagulls, wheeling and screaming in the sky, diving down to what must surely be the sea. All around her, things began to look familiar. Stunted pines grew now at the edge of the road, twisting up through tall grass and clumps of raggedy white flowers, and there were no hillsides. Everywhere the land was flat, just as she remembered it.

Puffs of white sand blew across the windswept road where she walked, and Minerva had to stop from time to time to lick the stuff out from between her toes. It was not a task she minded. Sand meant that a beach lay somewhere nearby, and beyond it the bay. In no time at all, she'd be home!

But when she finally crossed the road that ran along the edge of the beach, it was not the old familiar back road behind the boardwalk houses. It was a strange, deserted road with no houses at all, and no boardwalk. Tall, grassy dunes blocked her view of the sea, and it was not easy making her way over the shifting, sliding sand. But the fresh, tangy air kept her going, and all at once she was squinting out over sparkling blue water.

The beach was flat now, and Minerva was able to scamper her way across it, heading for the water's edge. She knew there was still a distance to go — this wasn't *her* beach — but if the tide happened to be out, she just might find herself some cracked-open mussels, or a crab or two with a broken shell. As always, Minerva was hungry, and the thought of all the tasty little creatures awaiting her down among the rocks made her mouth water.

But all of a sudden Minerva stopped short, discovering that this was not her calm, remembered bay at all. Huge, dark waves, all frothed with white, were rolling in, one after another, and crashing down on the sand with a thunderous roar. At home the waves were never like this, not even during the first vicious storms of autumn, and Minerva decided at once to forget all about crabs and mussels.

Scrambling her way to the top of a dune, far back on the beach, Minerva stood high, peering out over the angry water. In one direction she saw nothing but a few tiny, sunstruck islands, and beyond them a dim, faraway, gray line where the sea met the sky. In the other direction, a long, distant spit of land curved its way out into the pounding waves, sheltering whatever waters lay on the other side. There, thought Minerva, there just beyond it would be the gently rippling waves of her own bay.

Keeping close to the dunes, far away from the terrifying, crashing waves, Minerva set out at a steady pace, and by midafternoon she had reached the spit of land. It was far wider than it had looked from a distance — wide enough for roads and houses and trees — and she was a long time crossing to the other side. But all of a sudden, coming out from the cool shadows of a stand of pines, she found herself staring out over the calm blue water she remembered. Distant, weathered houses ringed the sunny beach — and just in front of them was a thin strip of brownish gray that must surely be the boardwalk!

Tired as she was, Minerva crossed the curving beach at a gallop, weaving her way among clusters of people under bright umbrellas, not stopping until she saw for sure that the strip of gray *was* the boardwalk. Breathing hard, she sat down for a moment to rest, moved slowly on, then climbed the splintery, well-remembered steps.

She was in no hurry now to find her own house. All she wanted to do was to roll around on the warm, familiar boards, deliciously scratching her back, and then to sit in the sun, looking out over the beach. The afternoon was glorious, and as always, there were crowds of children racing in and out of the water, dashing to and from the boardwalk for towels and buckets, calling to each other in shrill voices. Though one or two of them stopped at the edge of the boardwalk to reach up and give her a hasty, friendly pat, most of them didn't notice her at all.

When she felt rested, Minerva got up and began padding slowly along the boardwalk, studying the houses, searching for the porch railing that might be hers. She had passed no more than a dozen of them when all at once a small, vaguely remembered voice came floating to her over the sand.

"Hey, Mary Ellen! Look who's up there on the boardwalk! It's that stray cat I told you about, the one my dad hit the night we came here! At least I *think* it is."

"Patches!" Suddenly Mary Ellen was flying up the steps, swooping down on Minerva, gathering her up into her arms. "Oh, Patches, it's really you! How did you ever get here?"

"Are you sure it's the same one?" Leaning over the boardwalk, the little boy who had called out was staring intently up at Minerva. "I mean, how could it be? The doctor said the lady who adopted her lived someplace far away. So how could it be?"

"It is," Mary Ellen said positively. "I'd know Patches anywhere. I guess she just wanted to come home. Cats do that, you know."

"All that way?" The boy was incredulous. "But the doctor said — "

"I know," said Mary Ellen, sliding Minerva up over her shoulder and rocking her tenderly back and forth. "It must have been a long, long walk. Oh, Patches, I'm so glad you came home! We tried to find that lady after Danny came and told us about the accident, but the doctor didn't know where she lived, and she was already gone by the time we called up about you. I'm sorry, old Patches. There wasn't anything we could do."

"How did she *get* here, do you suppose?" Danny was still staring up at Minerva, a look of wonder in his eyes. "Could a lame old cat like that one really walk that far? How did she find her way?"

"This cat," said Mary Ellen, tickling Minerva behind the ears, "is very smart. She could find her way anywhere. Besides that, she's independent. She doesn't like to belong to anybody."

"Not even you?"

"Oh, sometimes — when she happens to feel like it. And I think she feels like it now. She's purring. Let's take her home, Danny, and get her something to eat. Poor thing — she's all skin and bones!"

Before long, Minerva was sharing a huge dish of Tastee Tidbits with Princess. After that she strolled around the house two or three times, checking to see whether her old pile of rags underneath was still there (it was) and that nothing was different. Satisfied, she curled up beside Princess on the porch railing, enjoying the last rays of afternoon sun, lazily watching Danny and Mary Ellen racing around with their friends on the beach below.

"It's good to be home," sighed Minerva. "I don't know when I've been so tired out."

"It must have been a long, hard walk," said Princess admiringly. "Honestly, I don't know how you managed to find your way."

"You know me," Minerva said proudly. "Never been lost a day in my life. Knew my way right from the start. The long walk wasn't the worst of it, by any means. The worst part was being locked up all the time, not being able to get out."

"Funny," mused Princess. "When I was lost I was *out* and wanted to be *in,* and when you were lost — "

"Not lost," Minerva reminded her, "just away."

"And when you were — away — you were *in* and wanted to be *out.*"

"I guess it takes all kinds," said Minerva. "There's a whole lot to be said for the house-cat life, and I'll have to admit that all the people I stayed with were good to me. You just can't imagine the marvelous food I had at Mrs. Weatherington's — but, oh, how I missed my freedom. There's a whole lot more to be said for the independent life, if you ask me."

"A little of each," suggested Princess. "That's the best way."

"Yes," said Minerva, drowsily stretching out her aching limbs, "and right this minute the housecat life suits me just fine. I may even sleep indoors for a while, just till I get myself in shape again."

"You won't have very long," said Princess. "The nights are getting chilly now, and when the nights get chilly, that means summer's nearly over. And then we'll all be going home."

"There's time," said Minerva, "still quite a bit of time. And I'll be my old peppy, independent self before you know it."

But to her own surprise, Minerva grew lazier and lazier, and as the last days of summer sped by, she found herself dreading the long, hard winter that lay ahead. Her gimpy leg gave her trouble on damp days, and though she knew that rainy weather was the very best time for mouse hunting, mostly she just lolled about before the fire instead. She was living almost the same sort of pampered, indoor life she'd had with Mrs. Weatherington, she often thought — but with an enormous difference. Here she could come and go as she pleased, in or out, and no one ever tried to stop her. She was entirely free, just the way she wanted to be.

The sky was overcast on the day Mary Ellen and her family began packing up the car, and as she sat watching from the back porch, Minerva felt as gray and lifeless as the sky above. Soon she'd be alone again, chasing around in the damp fields for her food, sleeping on the old pile of rags underneath the house, feeling aches and pains in her gimpy leg whenever it rained.

For the first time in all her independent life, Minerva knew that she would be lonely. Until this summer, human beings hadn't been much a part of her life, but as she watched Mary Ellen busily loading the car, not paying attention to her, she felt suddenly sorrowful. A whole long year would pass before she'd see her again — a whole year without being patted, tickled behind the ears, talked to. There'd be no more Tastee Tidbits, no saucers of milk, no cozy fires to warm her bones. There'd be nothing but the open fields, the sodden, windswept beach, the chilly pile of rags underneath the house.

When the car was packed, and Princess was perched on the ledge just below the back window, Minerva rose, stretched, and ambled over to the car to say good-bye. Mary Ellen, settled among the boxes and bags in the back seat, reached a hand out to her, fondly rubbing her whiskers.

"You can come if you like," she said softly, "or you can stay. It's up to you. Just remember that we won't be back until next summer — and that's a long, long time. Do you want to come?"

Backing slowly away from Mary Ellen's hand, meowing, Minerva stared out over the familiar fields behind the house, then up at the gray, stormy sky. Pretending that her decision was of no importance whatever, she sat down and began casually washing a back foot. And then, just as the car motor started up, she jumped lightly into the back seat and up to Mary Ellen's lap, not settling down, just perching. Slowly — waiting just long enough to be sure Minerva wasn't going to change her mind — Mary Ellen closed the door, then began gently patting her.

"You'll like it where we live," she murmured into Minerva's still perked ear. "It's all nice and woodsy, and there's even a brook, with tiny little crayfish in it. They're kind of like crabs, only skinnier, and Princess catches them all the time. You can too. And the backyard is huge, with great, big trees to climb, and we'll let you go out any old time you want to. In the winter we have fires in the fireplace every night, and you can sleep right in front of it if you want to. You'll like it where we live . . ."

Yes, thought Minerva, listening to the soft chattering of Mary Ellen's voice, chances were she would like it very much. Turning herself around a few times, she curled herself into a round, tight ball. Later she might jump up to the ledge beside Princess, and watch the scenery speeding past, but right now it was pleasant just drowsing a bit, thinking about catching crayfish in Mary Ellen's brook, and dozing before all those winter fires.

There was, she thought contentedly, a whole lot to be said for the housecat life.